This book belongs to:

- - - - - - - - - - - - - - - - - - -

For the wonderful Wayne Winstone and his words of wisdom.

With love.

K.S.

*Sir Charlie Stinky Socks would like to donate 10% of the royalties from
the sale of this book to Naomi House Children's Hospice.*

EGMONT

We bring stories to life

This edition first published in Great Britain 2012
Sir Charlie Stinky Socks and the Really Dreadful Spell first published 2010 by Egmont UK Limited
239 Kensington High Street, London W8 6SA

www.egmont.co.uk

Text and illustrations copyright © Kristina Stephenson 2010
Music copyright © Nigel Ellis 2012
Songs copyright © Mark Walker 2012
Recording copyright © Egmont UK Limited 2012

Kristina Stephenson, Nigel Ellis and Mark Walker have asserted their moral rights

ISBN 978 1 4052 6084 8

1 3 5 7 9 10 8 6 4 2

A CIP catalogue record for this title is available from the British Library

Printed and bound in Malaysia

46407/5

Sir Charlie Stinky Socks

and the Really DREADFUL Spell

Kristina Stephenson

EGMONT

Once up**o**n a
misty morning,
from the top of a
twisty-wisty beanstalk,
Someone was looking down . . .

. . . on to a tall, tall
tower (with a pointy roof)
in the middle of . . .

... a Magical Forest.

It was the day after a little
Princess's party and everyone
was happy there, when,
suddenly –
without any warning –
Someone ...

... cast a *spell!*

And over the Princess,
her favourite monster, and
a wily witch with a watch
(oh and everyone else in this magical world),
a **stony** silence fell!

Now...

...only a power mightier than magic
could break this *dreadful spell*
(*if* such a power could reach the tower
before the sands of time r a n o u t!).

But the only power that was strong enough was twenty
leagues from there – in the boots of a knight who'd
been at the party and was making his way back home.

Oh no!

Further away from the tower
went the power *until* . . .

… Sir Charlie Stinky Socks stopped.
Phew!
The bold, brave knight, and his faithful
cat, Envelope, wanted a bite to eat.
So Sir Charlie took out a slice of cake
(a piece he had brought from the Princess's party)
and with one quick flick of his
trusty sword he –

**Hang on a minute!
Hold this story!**

Where *was* his
trusty sword?

It was back in the tower, at the bottom of the stairs –
where he'd left it after the party.

Gadzooks!

"Never mind," said Sir Charlie. "I suppose lunch will just have to wait."
And he rallied his faithful (famished) cat and
mounted his groaning grey mare.

Clip clop, clip clop,

clippety clippety clop!

Back to the forest and the
tall, tall tower rode
Sir Charlie and his cat.

Oh, and his mighty power
went with him
(along with some wiggly woos).

Good job too!

For in the tall, tall tower
(with the pointy roof) time was . . .

running out!

The *mists* grew *mistier*.
Murkier too!

And some worrying signs in
the road suggested the
gallant knight
might be . . .

. . . lost!

WHERE'S THE TOWER?

HAVEN'T THE FOGGIEST!

Oh no !
Deep woe !
Which way to go?

Sir Charlie was about to find out.
For through that muddlesome
murky mist,
he saw **Someone**
heading his way.

Aha, thought Sir Charlie, a **mysterious stranger** pulling a heavy load!
Just the thing for a knight to meet at a moment such as this.

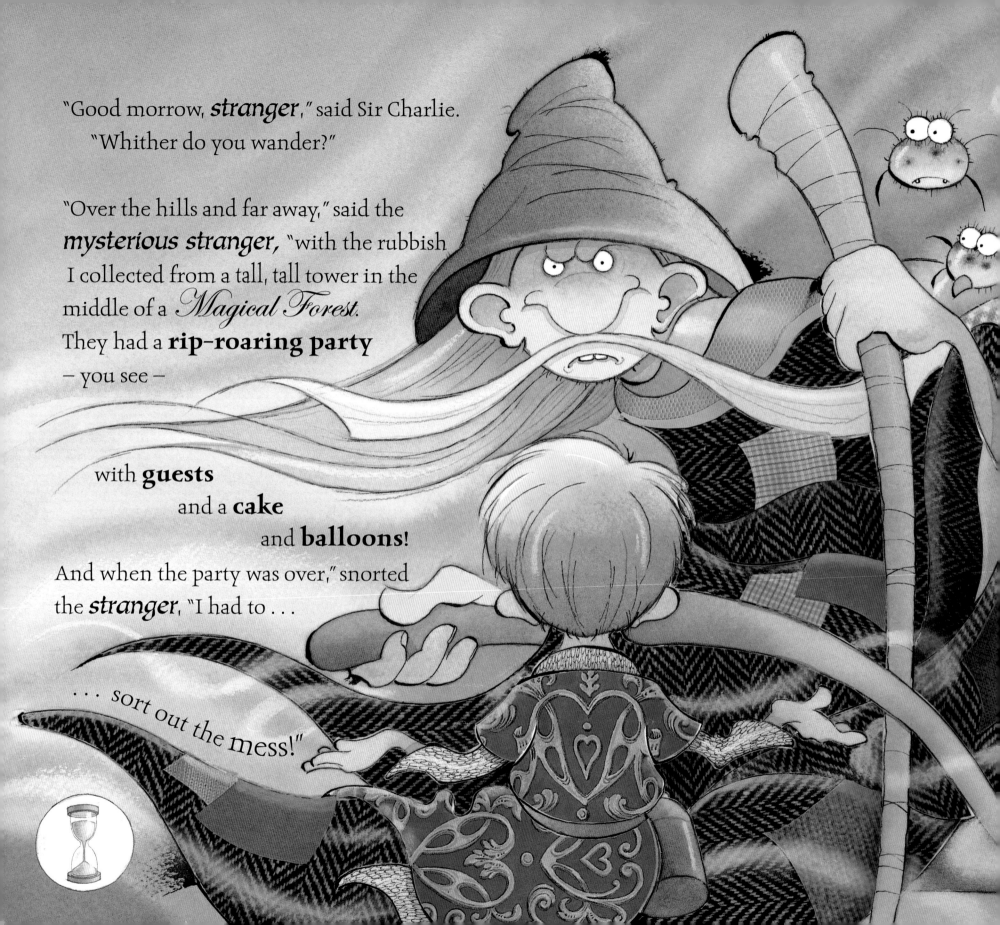

"Good morrow, *stranger*," said Sir Charlie.
"Whither do you wander?"

"Over the hills and far away," said the
mysterious stranger, "with the rubbish
I collected from a tall, tall tower in the
middle of a *Magical Forest*.
They had a **rip-roaring party**
– you see –

with **guests**
and a **cake**
and **balloons**!
And when the party was over," snorted
the **stranger**, "I had to . . .

. . . sort out the mess!"

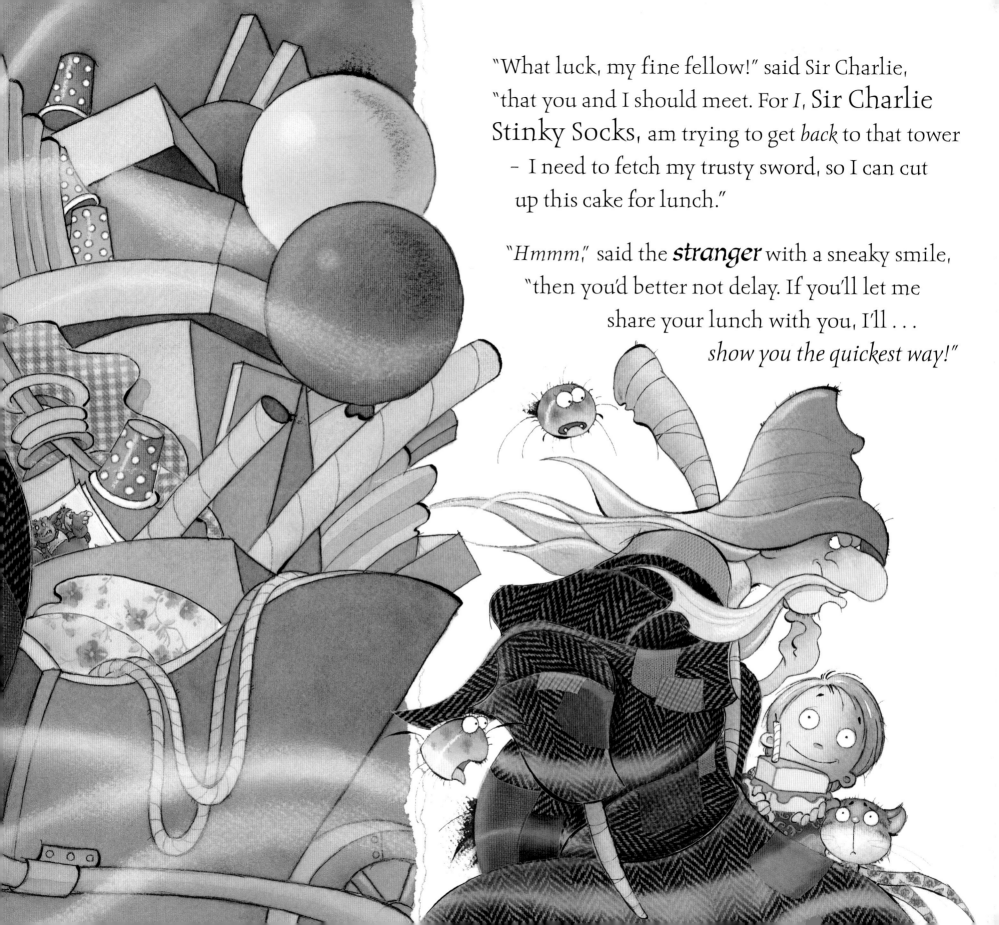

"What luck, my fine fellow!" said Sir Charlie,
"that you and I should meet. For *I*, Sir Charlie
Stinky Socks, am trying to get *back* to that tower
- I need to fetch my trusty sword, so I can cut
up this cake for lunch."

"*Hmmm*," said the **stranger** with a sneaky smile,
"then you'd better not delay. If you'll let me
share your lunch with you, I'll . . .
show you the quickest way!"

Sir Charlie harnessed his hungry horse to the stranger's cart full of rubbish and set off again through the *murky mists* on his journey back to the tower . . .

trit trot, trit trot, humpity lumpity bump!

. . . paying little heed to the worrying signs and the stranger's sneaky smile and not even *knowing* that in the tall, tall tower, time was . . .

r u n n i n g out!

. . . clever Sir Charlie did!
Yippee!
How odd then that the **mysterious**
stranger lost his sneaky smile while . . .

. . . a bubbling, burbling bog!
Yuck!

There was no way round it,
no way through it and no way now to go back!
Because by some horrible hand of fate
this bog was . . .

. . . **all around!**

Envelope *moaned.*

The grey mare *groaned.*

All hope of lunch was
s i n k i n g.

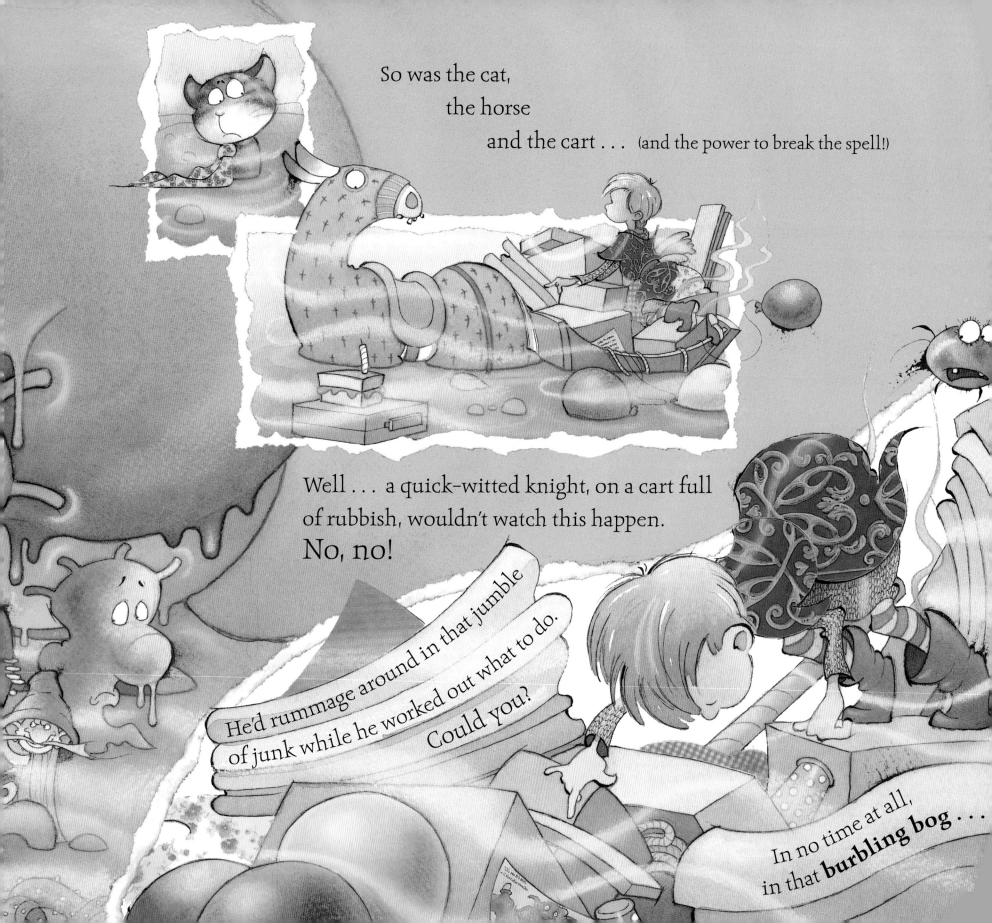

So was the cat,
   the horse
      and the cart . . .   (and the power to break the spell!)

Well . . . a quick-witted knight, on a cart full
of rubbish, wouldn't watch this happen.
No, no!

He'd rummage around in that jumble
of junk while he worked out what to do.
Could you?

In no time at all,
in that **burbling bog** . . .

At last they
were back in the
Magical Forest
where things looked . . .

decidedly different!

For in front of our troupe of tiring travellers was . . .

slappety squelch,
    slappety squelch,
        splodge, splodge, splodge!

. . . Sir Charlie Stinky Socks
(and his mighty power) drew closer
to the tall, tall tower. The knight ignored
the worrying signs and the anxious
wiggly woos and followed the lead of the
mysterious stranger who guided them
thoughtfully through
    that **burbling bog**
        and the *murky mist*
            to the middle of . . .

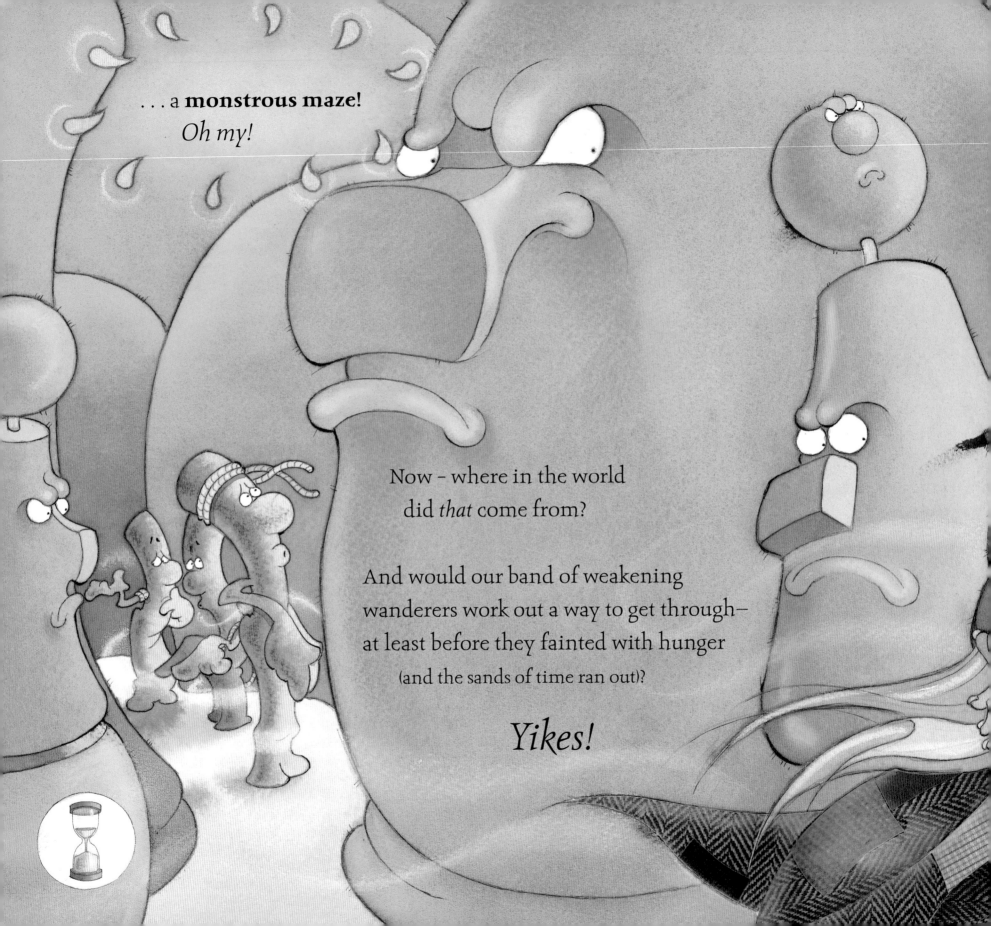

...a **monstrous maze!**

Oh my!

Now – where in the world
did *that* come from?

And would our band of weakening
wanderers work out a way to get through–
at least before they fainted with hunger
(and the sands of time ran out)?

Yikes!

... found the way out of that **monstrous maze** back to the tall, tall tower and the *twisty-wisty beanstalk* and . . .

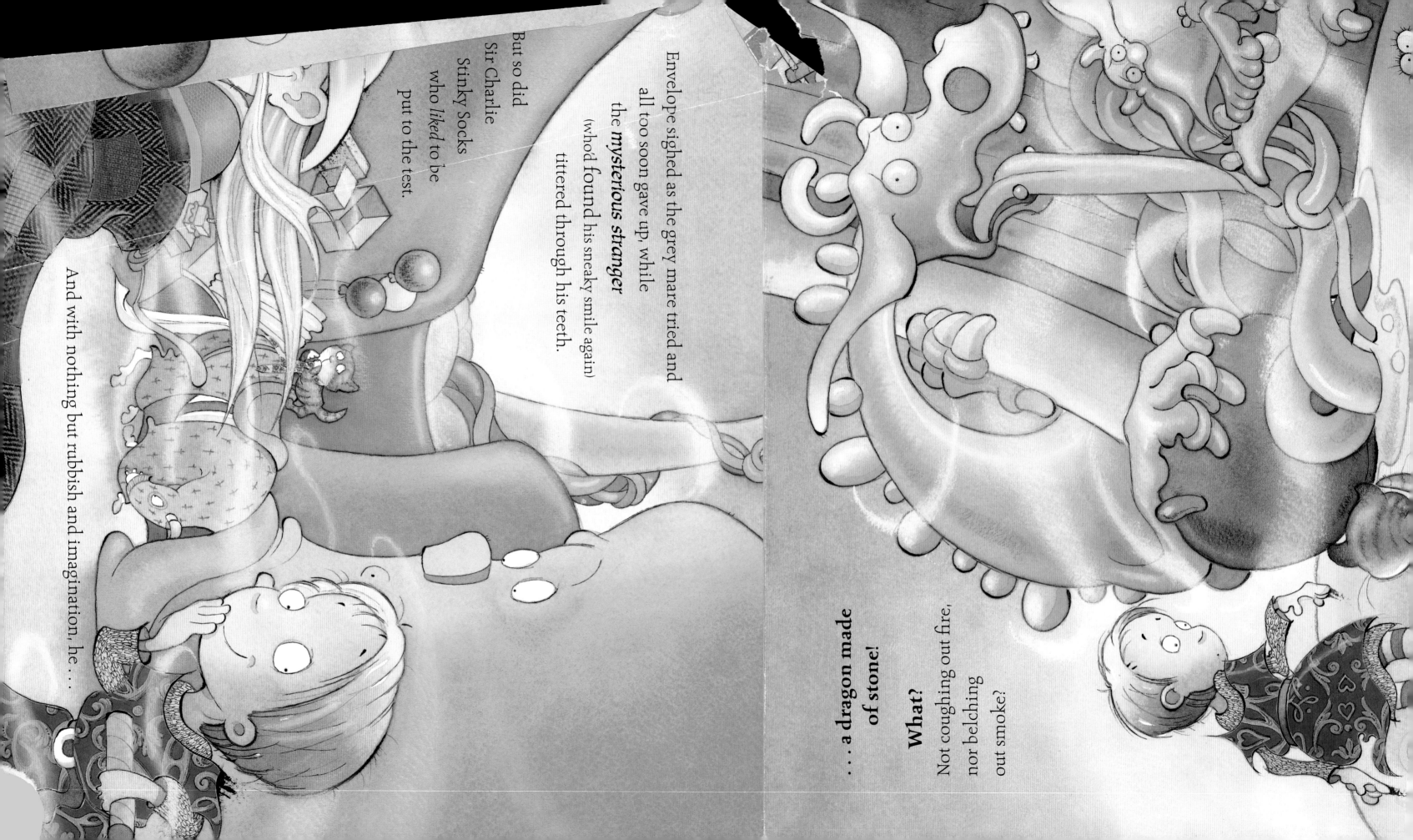

Envelope sighed as the grey mare tried and all too soon gave up, while the *mysterious stranger* (who'd found his sneaky smile again) tittered through his teeth.

But so did Sir Charlie Stinky Socks who *liked* to be put to the test.

And with nothing but rubbish and imagination, he . . .

. . . a dragon made of stone!

What?

Not coughing out fire, nor belching out smoke?

Terrible piercing **spikes** they were,
pushing Sir Charlie back – *back* to
the farthest limb of the *beanstalk*
where he teetered on the brink.

. . . he kicked off his boots,
whipped off his socks and
wafted them in the air!

Wow! The powerful pong from those
pungent stockings . . .

. . . *withered the thorns away!*

**Hey
hey!**

"Ha ha," said Sir Charlie. "My stinky socks are mightier than the sword!"

...the **mysterious stranger**,

roaring with laughter at the top of the tower

where time was

a l m o s t

o u t !

Up the twisty-wisty beanstalk scrambled Sir Charlie Stinky Socks - right to the top of the tall, tall tower where ...

...*something* made him
STOP!

But who could have cast it?
Well, can't you guess?

Yes! **Yes!** **Yes!**

First there was the mist, then there was the bog and of course the **monstrous maze.**

All together the worrying signs pointed to ...

"Think!" said Sir Charlie Stinky Socks.
And he didn't need to think *twice*.

With a **wooshity thwack** of his trusty sword he –

Hang on a second!
Have you forgotten?

He didn't *have* his sword!

That lusty blade was *inside* the tower
while the desperate knight was . . .

. . . *without.*
Nooooo!

Envelope *gasped.*

The grey mare gulped.

But Sir Charlie didn't think thrice . . .

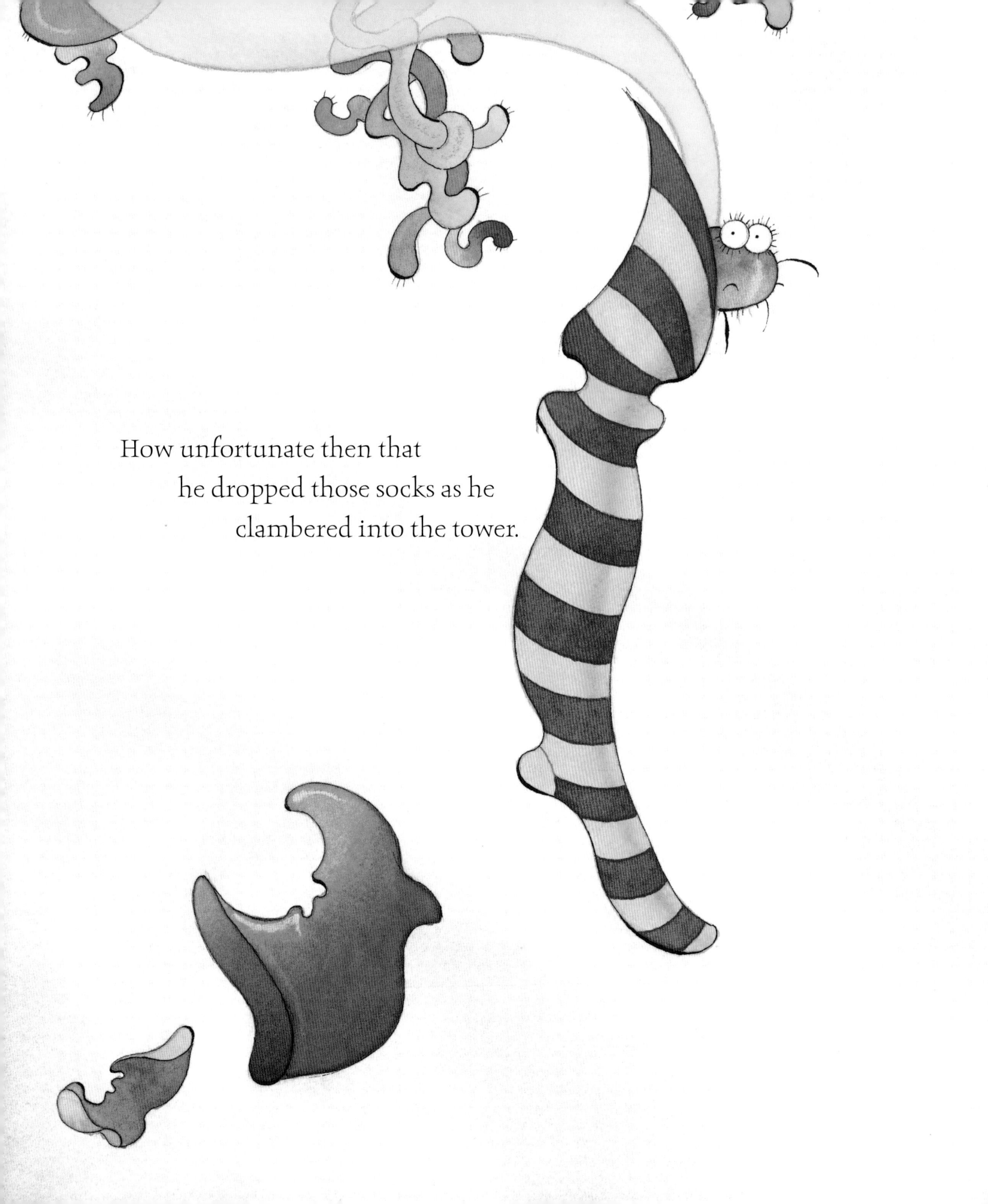

How unfortunate then that
he dropped those socks as he
clambered into the tower.

Three stone figures –
silent and still – stood
in the middle of
the room where the
mysterious stranger
(with the sneaky smile)
revealed what he
really was.

A wizard, of course – who'd been in disguise – now *that* would explain a lot!

"So! Little Stinky Socks!" he boomed at Sir Charlie. "You made it to the tower! You got through my **mist**, my **bog**, my **maze**, and even my **piercing thorns**. But here, my fearless, foolish friend, you'll meet your match in **me** – the most powerful Wizard that ever there was from the top of the twisty beanstalk.

I have bewitched the creatures in the forest and your friends in this tall, tall tower."

"Why?" said Sir Charlie to the wicked wizard. "What did they do to *you*?"

"They had a **rip-roaring part**
So I turned them all to **ston**
can turn them back
than magic car
get it?" sneered
"That powe
but the
of the
is about
out

of course, but they didn't invite me!

– see? – and not even *you* my brave little knight again. Because, only a power mightier break this **dreadful spell**. And don't you the wicked wizard.

is in your socks . . .

are at the bottom

tower and time

to run

Ha!"

No point arguing with an angry wizard – at least not at a time like this. If Sir Charlie were going to save his friends he'd have to . . .

... take **the blame!**

"I brought everyone to the Princess's party," said the honest knight. "If anyone here should be turned to stone, I think it should be me."

How tragic then for Sir Charlie Stinky Socks that the Wizard was quick to agree.

And that was that in the tall, tall tower,

A happily ever after!

Sir Charlie Stinky Socks hugged his cat and patted his good grey mare.

"'Twas a job well done!" he said to them.

"Now - are you ready for *another* adventure?"

THE END?